MW01488196

the Journey's End

JOHN EUDY

For G.K. Chesterton.

I wish I possessed half your wit, imagination, and talent.

Special thanks to Janelle, Trina, and my beautiful wife, Julie.

Copyright © 2023 John Eudy
All rights reserved.

Contents

Introduction

In a child's mind, everything exists in the world, and anything is possible; i.e., the world is full of possibilities. For example, as a young boy, I would wear old Army clothes, crawl along the ditch next to our house, and pretend to shoot at the birds flying overhead with my toy guns. Who else was gonna shoot down those enemy bombers? I also have fond memories of my grandma safety-pinning a bath towel around my neck and letting me run through the house in my Batman Underoos pretending to fight villains. You're hearing the '60 TV theme song right now, aren't you? I even remember wrapping a big piece of fabric around me like a cloak and wandering through the woods behind the house with a wooden sword pretending to be Galahad on his quest to find the Holy Grail.

Not too long ago, the incomparable G.K. Chesterton helped me recall all those old memories of high adventure from my boyhood. I was reading his essay *The Madhouse and the Nursery* (initially published in the Illustrated London News, Oct. 15, 1921.) when I came across something that caused me to laugh out loud. He wrote, "For instance, there are new schools where children are taught to play at being politicians. They are no longer left to play at being pirates, that infinitely more hounourable trade."

This story you're about to read was inspired by the previous quote and this one, "Of a sane man there is only one definition. He is a man who can have tragedy in his heart and comedy in his head." (Quoted from Kevin Belmonte's book *The Quotable Chesterton: The Wit and Wisdom of G.K. Chesterton,* published in 2011 by Thomas Nelson).

Therefore, this story is inspired by and dedicated to the hounourable G.K. Chesterton. Thank you, good sir, for your many exceptional works.

Chapter 1:
Alexander the Great

Alex lies in bed with his eyes closed. *It has to be a dream.* He thinks to himself over and over. Then, finally, the sickly youth opens his eyes, and seeing the familiar sights of his hospital room; he sighs loudly with disappointment.

"You okay, son?" asks his father. Alex turns his head to the left to see his mom and dad sitting next to him. Both are happy he is awake.

"I guess, dad." He says, turning his head back to the right to stare out the window. "I was just hopin' it was all a dream that I'd wake up in my own bed." There is a long pause. "Just kinda tired of bein' in this hospital."

"I know, Alex, I know. But, believe me, son, your mother and I would love to get you back home." He pats Alex's arm.

The boy skylarks out the window. "Sure looks nice out there. Wish I could go outside; play pirates, fight dragons, you know, go on an adventure or something?" He feels his mother's gentle touch on his left hand, the one with the I.V. in it.

His father stands and leans over him to brush his hair back. "Me too, son, me too. You have the best imagination of any kid I know. Your mother and I always love watchin' you play."

Alexander McBain is nine years old. He has a head full of wavy brown hair, dark green eyes, and a few freckles running across his nose. A typical boy from a small, midwestern American town, he was bold, adventurous, and highly imaginative. He has spent many summer afternoons playing with the other boys in the neighborhood. He and his friends enjoyed playing hotbox in the vacant lot down the street and riding their bikes to the public pool on the outskirts of town. When they weren't doing that, they would go on 'expeditions' in the creek behind their house and shoot their bows and bb guns in the field beyond. Alex also enjoyed catching tadpoles and crawdads in the brook or playing with his action figures and toy cars on the banks. Unfortunately, he hasn't been to the creek for some time now. Instead, he's been bedridden in the hospital, suffering from a disease that weakens him.

His dad sees the despondent stare in his son's sunken eyes, so he decides to break the uncomfortable silence with a story. "Son, you know why I gave you the name Alex?"

Alex turns to look at his dad; his curiosity is peaked. "No, dad. Why?"

"As a boy, I was fascinated by Alexander the Great's conquests. Do you know who he is?"

"No."

"Well, he was a great warrior from Greece. He fought many battles in many countries. From Persia down to Egypt."

"Where the mummies are?" Alex interrupts excitedly.

"Yes. He even won lands from Mesopotamia all the way over to India. He conquered the known world as a young man only in his 20s."

"Wow!"

"That made me want to go into the world and make my mark. Until I met your mother, that is." He turns to smile at her. "A Mediterranean beauty herself." He turns back to his son and winks.

"C'mon, Dad. No mushy stuff."

"Anyway, she gave me you. Ever since then, **you** have been my greatest adventure. I have always been amazed by you."

"Is'at why you call me Alex the Great sometimes?" he asks with a smile.

"No, I call you Alex the Great 'cause you are the greatest gift I've ever been given. You have always brought me great joy." He places his hand on his son's shoulder and looks deep into his eyes. "I have and always will be proud of you, son. And I'm sure you'll conquer this illness too."

"I'll do my best, Dad."

"I know you will, my boy." Alex's parents know that what he suffers from is terminal. But, whether out of hope for a miracle or a desire to keep his spirits up, they have agreed not to discuss it with him yet. His dad works daily and can only be by his side evenings and weekends. His mother is with him most days. Alex is delighted when they are both with him, like today.

Aidan and Abila's marriage is somewhat unique. Neither of their families saw it coming; an American Protestant man marrying a Lebanese Catholic woman. It certainly stirred some heated discussions among family members. Even now, Alex has noticed his grandmother, Sitti, as she is affectionately known, scowling at his dad occasionally. His youthful naivety prevented him from understanding why, but he always shrugged it off because he loved his parents as equally and unconditionally as they loved him.

Aidan will often leave the room when Alex sleeps. He usually finds a secluded place outside the hospital to discuss his son's condition with God. On the other hand, Abila stays by his side and prays her rosary unceasingly. Alex has woken to her beautiful prayers before, which always lifts his spirits.

This Sunday is no exception, either. It has been a fantastic day for Alex. He enjoyed the company of his parents, grandparents, and friends who stopped by. He watched cartoons on the TV while his mom fed him lunch. "Hospital food can be so gross." He sometimes protests. Yet he always eats as much of it as possible, especially when Sitti has smuggled in a sweet treat. Of course, nothing to upset his vitals, just something to let him know she cares.

It's growing late, though, and they have all departed for the night. Alex is tired after such a busy day. He nods off while his favorite nurse, Mrs. Bonnie, takes his vitals and completes her paperwork. He knows she won't be back for quite a while after this, so he has grown accustomed to falling asleep then. What he doesn't know is that this night is different.

Hospital nights are never truly quiet. Monitors are beeping; nurses are coming and going, and cries and conversations from neighboring patients have woken him before. Tonight, however, an unknown sound startles young Alex awake. His room is dark and still, more silent than he is used to. He looks around and is shocked to discover a stranger sitting beside him. The man has a peculiar glow about him, like he makes his own light, which causes Alex to study him briefly. The man appears tall, seated with his elbow on his knees and leaning toward Alex's bed. He is clean-shaven and about the same age as his dad. The visitor is wearing a clean, dark-blue suit with a gray waistcoat and gold-colored tie. His shirt is probably the brightest white Alex has ever seen. His facial features are unique; Alex can't tell what race he is. His hair is dark brown, wavy, and a little long, just about to touch his shoulders. Regardless, the stranger waits until he knows the boy has finished inspecting him before saying, "Peace be with you, young Alexander."

Alex has deduced where this man has come from somewhere in the deep recesses of his young mind. "Are...are you an angel?" He asks nervously.

"Yes. How very perceptive of you," He says as he stands. "My name is Præsidiel. I am here to...."

"Wait," Alex interrupts, "does this mean I'm dead?" he asks in a panic as he pats his body and visually examines himself.

Præsidiel chuckles. "No, young Alexander, you are not dead yet."

"Phew." He pushes himself up in bed. "I'm sorry, Mr. Præsidiel, I didn't mean to interrupt. Yuh just caught me off guard there."

The angel smiles. "It is forgiven. However, I am here with a message. First, may I ask, are you aware your illness is terminal?" He questions with a somber tone.

"I, uh. What's 'terminal' mean?"

"It means your illness will claim your life; sadly, you will die."

Alex slumps his shoulders. "Well, no one has **actually** told me that before. But I could tell it wasn't good by the looks on everyone's faces and some o' the talk I've overheard."

"Are you prepared for what is to come, Alexander?"

"Can I tell you the truth?" Alex thinks about his question for a split second and mumbles, "What am I thinkin'? You're an angel; you'd know if I was lying anyways." He looks to the angel, "No sir, I'm not ready for what I think happens next. Oh, uh, don't get me wrong; I'd be excited to meet Jesus an' all. It's just...well, I'm a bit scared." He begins to wring his hands. "See, I don't want to make my parents sad or anything, neither."

"Alexander, our Lord has heard your mother's prayers, your father's ... opinions, and even your desire for a backyard adventure too." The angel pauses. "You know the story *A Christmas Carol*, yes?"

"Oh, yes, sir." Alex's eyes light up. "Mom 'n dad watch the cartoon movie with me every year. I like it when Scrooge turns nice. I sometimes feel like Tiny Tim without the crutch. Unfortunately, I'm stuck in this hospital too."

"Good. You will appreciate this then. Our Lord has sent me to take you on a different quest for the next few nights so you might live life to the fullest before joining him for the greatest of all adventures. This will also afford you more time with your family before you depart."

"So, I still have tuh die, then?" Alex asks sadly.

"Yes, child. Everyone must." Alex turns his eyes downward. "However, Our Lord awaits you; nothing is greater than being with him in paradise."

Alex exhales a deep breath. "Okay, Mr. Præsidiel, I trust you … and God." He looks back up at the angel. "So, z'is mean you'll be back tomorrow night, then?"

"Yes."

"Can I tell my mom 'n dad you came to see me?"

"Yes."

"Gotta tell yuh, sir, I don't know how you're gonna do it, but I'm kinda excited about gettin' out o' this bed and goin' on an adventure. So where're we goin' first?"

"All in good time, young Alexander. All in good time. For now, you must rest."

"Okay. I am kinda tired anyway." Alex says, sliding back down into the hospital bed. "Do I need to say my prayers again?"

"No." says the angel. He pulls the boy's blanket up, covering and tucking him in. "Our Lord has heard your prayer and intends to take and keep your soul." He grins at Alex. "He has sent me to guide your ways until then." Alex returns his smile before falling fast asleep. It will be the deepest sleep he's had in quite some time.

* * * * *

Alex wakes the following day to the sound of his parents whispering. "Morning, Momma.

Morning, Dad." He says, carefully rubbing his eyes and avoiding tangling the I.V. tube.

"Good morning, my darling," his mother sings.

"Morning, son. How'd you sleep last night?" Asks his dad.

"Great!" exclaims Alex bolting up in his bed. He extends his scrawny arms, stretching in the morning light beaming through the window.

"Wow." His dad chuckles. "You sure are bright-eyed and bushy-tailed this morning."

After a prolonged yawn, Alex begins to chatter, "Mom, Dad, you won't believe it, but an angel came to see me last night. Said his name was Pra...Pray...sidiel? Cool, huh? Can't believe I got to meet a real angel."

"An angel, huh?" Aidan asks with skepticism. Alex's mother slaps her husband's arm, scolding him with a look.

Alex is unphased. "He said he was gonna take me on a different adventure each night this week before...." Alex's voice trails off when he suddenly realizes he is about to confess his fatal prognosis. Sadness overwhelms him. Alex's mother reads his sudden emotional change; tears well up in her eyes. She knows her son all too well and can see he understands his fate.

Aidan, contrarily, grows angry. He thinks someone has informed his son without consulting him. "Son, who told you this? Was it a doctor, a nurse?"

"No, Dad, it was the angel. We talked about things, and he said it was almost time to go see Jesus."

"I'll find out who was in here last night." He growls before abruptly departing the room.

Alex feels like he has done something wrong. "You believe me don't you, Momma?"

"If you believe it's true, Alex, then yes, I believe you." She tries to be more encouraging and comforting. She leans over his bed and hugs him. "Please forgive your dad and me. We're scared and don't want anything more to happen to you." A tear escapes down her cheek. She stands back up and discreetly wipes it away.

"It's true, Momma. It really was an angel."

Aidan returns a short while later. His quest to find the one who revealed the horrible truth to his son was unsuccessful. However, his conscience drives him back to visit his only son before he must head off to work. Abila stays by her son's side most of the day. She comes and goes as necessary but is always there to help Alex eat and speak with the doctor when he checks in.

The day eventually closes out in the usual silence. Nurse Bonnie left the curtains half open so Alex could fall asleep on his side while staring out at the night sky.

Chapter 2:
Alex the Firefighter

Alex feels someone grasping his left shoulder and gently shaking him. "Come on. Wake up, Alexander! There is no time to waste." The boy rolls over to see a fully dressed fireman staring at him. "Get up. Get dressed. Can you not hear the alarm bells?"

Dazed and confused, Alex looks around. He is not in the hospital anymore. Instead, he's in an upper room with a brass pole in the corner and bunks on either side. "What time is it?" He rubs his eyes. *That's strange*, he thinks. He has grown used to I.V. tubes getting stuck in a blanket and pulling at his arm, but he doesn't feel that. He looks down and sees he's in his pajamas, not the hospital gown. There are no tubes or wires connected to him, either.

"Hurry up and get your gear on!" Yells the man who woke Alex up. "We will be in fire truck number one." He jumps to the pole and quickly slides out of sight.

"Is this the adventure Præsidiel promised?" He wonders out loud.

A few moments later, Alex comes sliding down the pole. Running in boots two sizes too big, he clomps toward the firetruck. A firefighter's coat drags the ground behind him while he keeps shoving the oversized helmet up on his head so he can see where he's going. Then, finally arriving at the truck, he recognizes the person holding the door open for him. "Mr. Præsidiel!" He exclaims.

The angel chuckles at the boy's appearance.

"What? This's the smallest I could find back there."

"I guess it will do, young Alexander. It will do." The angel approves. Alex shuffles up into the truck. "By the way, you may call me Mr. Ray for short."

"You got it, Mr. Ray." Replies Alex as he slides over in the seat.

Mr. Ray climbs in and settles on the seat. He leans to Alex and asks, "I heard this fire is hellish; are you ready for it?" The truck lurches forward. The sirens begin to wail while red and blue lights illuminate the night.

"Yessir. Jus' hand me a hose when we git there and point me in the right direction." He answers boldly. "I'll put that fire out, fur sure."

Mr. Ray looks heavenward and grins widely.

* * * * *

The driver turns off the sirens just before they arrive. He slows the truck to a crawl before stopping on the side of the house. Alex gets his first, up close, and personal look at a real-life inferno. Fire belches from a broken window, curling up and around the roof line in a steady stream. Vinyl siding melts away while wood buckles. Flames dance on the roof as they turn the house to smoke. He can see through the wall studs in one area. He mumbles, "Boy, looks hot as a pizza oven in there."

"Again, are you sure you are ready for this?" Mr. Ray asks one more time.

The fight-or-flight urge battles deep within Alex's rapidly beating heart. Though fear grips him, he thinks, *I gotta be brave. God gave me this adventure, so I gotta show Him I can do this.* He swallows hard. "Yessir,"–his voice cracks slightly–"I'm ready." He flings open the door, jumps out, and asks, "Where's the hose?"

Mr. Ray leads him to the side of the house, untouched by the fire. There he unreels a garden hose and hands the business end to Alex. "Here you go. You are the lead nozzleman."

Alex eagerly takes it without hesitation, rounds the corner, and points it at the burning building. He twists the nozzle back and forth, but no water comes out. He looks behind him at Mr. Ray, who shrugs his shoulders. "Little help," Alex yells. One of the other firefighters turns the spigot on while a playful sigh slips past Mr. Ray's lips.

Mr. Ray nudges Alex to move into the burning building. A thick, black smoke greets them when they enter the front door. Flames climb the walls and lick at the door jam. The boy can barely see the hallway past the living room through the smoldering fog. They move forward. Alex is indiscriminately spraying everything around the living room. Mr. Ray pats him on the shoulder and shouts, "Make a path to the hallway. We must check the rooms for survivors."

"Okay." He begins soaking the area directly in front of them and cautiously following his stream of water.

Upon reaching the hallway, something at the end of the hall catches his eye. There is a giant face within the flames. It is a red, snarling, devilish face. Spiraling horns of fire protrude from it. Its mouth opens, and it appears to be screaming something, but whatever it's yelling goes unheard. Alex tries to focus on spraying the walls, floor, and ceiling in front of them while cautiously approaching the terrifying face.

The boy stops within a few feet of the thing on the wall. The heat in the confined space is intensifying. He stands upright and cocks his head to the side. Though he listens intently, he still can't understand what the face is saying. "Psshh!" He says in a dismissive tone, "I don't have time fer you." He turns the hose nozzle straight into the mouth of the flaming face. It sputters and gurgles, dissipating into a cloud of white steam. The bulk of the fire sizzles away with it. "Cough...cough." Alex waves his hand in the air trying to dispel the sulfuric fumes. "Man, it smells like rotten eggs." He yells while turning to look at Mr. Ray. He laughs before saying, "Just like them clowns at the fair. You know, yuh squirt 'em to make the balloon fill up an' pop?"

Mr. Ray shakes his head and smiles. Then, turning more serious, he points to the closed door next to them. "Go on, kick in the door," he shouts. "We must clear the house."

"I don't think I'm big 'nough for that."

"Yes, you are. God has given you the strength you need. Quickly, kick down the door! Get in there and clear the room."

"Oookay." Alex kicks as hard as he can at the door with his oversized boot heel. To his surprise, it cracks around its edges and falls to the ground. Smoke billows out of the dark room, filling the ceiling overhead. Alex looks down at his feet. *Wow, can't believe that actually worked*, he thinks.

"Alexander." Prompts Mr. Ray.

"Oh, yeah." He turns and hands his nozzle to his partner. Taking out his flashlight, he shines it around the smoke-filled room. He spots a man lying on the floor. The man is weak but conscious. Without a second thought, Alex rushes to his side. He lifts the man's arm over his shoulders and pulls him out. The man regains enough consciousness to stagger alongside Alex.

Together they make it back through the smoldering hallway and out the front door. Alex helps the man sit on the edge of the porch and then rushes back into the house. He yanks on the hose and yells, "He's out. Let's go."

"Roger, backing out." Responds Mr. Ray. Alex helps walk the hose back, leading his nozzleman out of the burning house. Once outside, Mr. Ray shuts off his nozzle while Alex helps the man stand. Another group of firemen rushes in with hoses to contain the flames erupting from the charred home. Paramedics receive the man from Alex, escorting him to an ambulance.

Mr. Ray pats Alex on the back, "You did very well, young man."

Alex removes his oversized hat and wipes the sweat and soot from his forehead. "Thank you, Mr. Ray." Out of breath but very excited, he exclaims, "You see me kick that door down? That was awesome!" Alex and his angel rest long enough for the boy to catch his breath.

"We have a few moments, Alexander; maybe you better check in on the man you rescued." He nods in the direction of the ambulance.

"Oh. Yessir. I'll go check in on him."

Alex walks over, his coat tail dragging behind him. Then, bashfully, he approaches the man sitting in the back of the ambulance. "Uh, hi. My name's Alex. What's yours, mister?"

"Alasdair." He coughs. "Al...cough, cough...for short." The man takes a good long look at the boy. "Aren't you...cough...a bit young to be a firefighter?"

"Yessir, I probably am. I've pretended to be one many times before, though, so it's okay. I knew what I was doin'."

"Well...cough, cough...you did a great job, son. Thank you for savin' me."

"No problem, Mr. Al." The paramedics return to treating the man. "Well, sir, I better get back with my teammate. The paramedics'll take good care of you." Mr. Al nods his gratitude. "God bless you, sir." A tear appears in the corner of the man's eye. Alex nods back and then heads toward the fire truck.

"Woo, it was hot in there, huh?" Mr. Ray asks. "A real baptism by fire."

Alex sits down and places his helmet on the ground in front of him. "Yessir, it was." They watch the rest of the firefighters tamp down the blaze until the half-standing house is a smoldering, black mess. The young firefighter has a bit of a confused and worried look. "So, what was that...thing? In the fire?" He asks, his voice trailing off at the end.

"That was the face of the evil one, Alexander, the adversary."

"Oh." Alex grows silent for a moment. "Then how...?"

"Good thing I was holding on to the hose, huh? The devil cannot stand holy water." Mr. Ray says with a wide grin.

"Wait, what?" Alex looks up at Præsidiel, who winks and smiles at him.

"Never forget, young man. I am your guardian angel."

"Oh. Oh yeah." He smiles to himself. "You holding onto the hose turned it into holy water. Huh."

"We saved more than a man's life tonight, my young friend. We may have just saved his soul as well." Alex scratches his head in confusion. Mr. Ray slaps the tops of his legs and says, "Well, we cast out the most unclean and saved a soul. All in a good night's work, yes?" He lets out a deep sigh. "Unfortunately, it is time to get you back."

"Back? To the hospital?" Alex turns his head downward. "Aww, man. Do I have to go back?"

"Yes, I am afraid you do...for now." Mr. Ray motions to the red pickup truck. "We will take the truck back while the rest finish up here. Come on, get in."

Alex reluctantly climbs in. He takes off his coat and wads it up. *I am feeling kinda tired after all that*, he thinks. He places the coat between his head and the door and then leans against it. It's surprisingly comfortable. Mr. Ray drives them toward the hospital while the boy quickly falls asleep.

Chapter 3:
Sir Alex, the Brave

The next day he wakes in his hospital bed. He is sad at first. All the tubes and wires have been reconnected to his body; he hears the familiar beeping of the heart monitor. Sitting in his bed alone, he thinks about how he will explain everything that happened. *How in the world did I get out of these tubes and wires? Who put 'em all back in? I sure hope Mrs. Bonnie won't be mad at me for that.*

His mood brightens, though, as soon as his parents arrive. He tells them about the burning house, the scary face, squirting water in its mouth, and saving Mr. Al. He is so excited about telling the story that his heart monitor beeps faster. Concerned, one of the nurses charges into the room mid-story to check on him. Then, realizing he is okay, she stays to hear how his tale ends.

"Wow, that was some dream." She states.

"No, ma'am. That wasn't a dream. That was real. I was sweating and everything." Alex looks down at his dry robe. "Huh. Must've changed when we got back." He mutters.

"Mmm, hmm." The nurse doubts. "I'll be back in a while with your meds, Alex."

"Mom. Dad. You believe me, don'tcha?"

"I don't know, son." Hesitates his dad. "How'd you get the I.V. out or fool the monitors? Not to mention getting out of the hospital." He smiles at Alex. "You've always been a very imaginative boy, so I think you had a fantastic,"–he nods, trying to reassure him–"and very realistic feeling dream. And that's great. I'm glad you did, right, mommy?" She smiles.

Deflated, Alex's expression turns downward.

"I'm sorry, son."–his dad says, looking at his watch–"I wish I could stay longer, but I need to get to work." He steps to his son's side and caresses the side of his head. "I do love you. Be brave, like the time you pretended to be a knight exploring that old dungeon. You remember? The basement?" He winks at Alex. "I'll see you as soon as I get off work." He kisses Alex on the forehead and then leaves quietly.

Alex looks at his mother, sitting calmly with her hand on his shin. "Mom?"

"Yes, honey."

"Do you think it was real or a dream?"

"Oh, my darling. I want so much for it to be real. I'm just not sure." She rubs his shin before stepping closer to him. She spots soot on his earlobe on the other side of his head. "Alex,"– she licks her thumb and reaches to clean it off– "how in the world did you manage to get dirt on your ear?" She stops her line of questioning when she remembers the story he just told.

"Told yuh, Mom, I really did help fight a fire last night."

At first, Abila doesn't know what to say. She thinks quietly for a moment. "I know. I'll ask nurse Bonnie to keep an extra eye on you tonight to check on you often. She'll find out if you're being whisked away or not. Okay?"

He perks up a little. "Okay, Momma."

* * * * *

As usual, Aidan returns in the evening to spend time with Alex. Unfortunately, the evening passes quickly. It isn't long before nurse Bonnie reminds everyone that it's quiet time. She completes her checks as the little family says their goodnights and goodbyes. "I'll be back to check on you soon." She assures. "Your mother told me to keep both eyes on you tonight, Alex. Mmm-hmm." She gives a playful nod to Alex, who gives her a 'thumbs-up.' Weak and tired, the boy slips into a deep slumber after she is gone.

"Wake up, Commander! You must wake up."

Alex bolts up in his bed. His head is spinning; he feels like he just closed his eyes. His body also feels extraordinarily heavy, weighted down. He lifts his hands and again notices all the tubes and wires are gone, but to his surprise, he realizes he is wearing a suit of chain mail. He looks to his left. Præsidiel is there. He wears a black surcoat with a white Hospitaller cross over his chest. He holds a black helmet with a white cloth turban around its crown. Alex looks down to find the same tunic adorns his chest.

Before he can ask any questions, Præsidiel debriefs him, "We have little time, Commander. A serpent has trapped the princess and several fair maidens in the hospital tower."

"A serpent?" He asks, flinging the blanket off his legs.

"Yes."

"Does it have wings and claws like the ones I've seen in books?"

"No. However, this serpent is still as fierce as the ones you have read about."

Alex jumps to his feet and searches for his sword. He spies it leaning in an old wooden chair. He grabs his sword belt, secures it around his waist, and inspects his stone-walled chamber, lit by torches. *Not in the hospital anymore*, he thinks as he smiles to himself. He grabs his round and somewhat battered shield. "Where is this snake then?"

Præsidiel continues to brief Alex as they make for the door, "It surrounds the tall spire next to the keep. The princess is trapped there."

"Well, let's go rescue 'em." Alex grins with excitement before dashing out of his chamber. His heart beats with excitement as he runs down the torchlit passageway. The chinking sound of his armor echoes off the stone walls. He feels his sheathed sword banging against his thigh. He can't wait to draw it against the serpent. It isn't long before he rushes beneath a stone archway and out into the courtyard. There he stops and takes in the scene.

The serpent's long, scaly body slithers slowly around the central spire, ascending to the enclosed parapet. Dark red spots run down its rust-colored back. Its scales shimmer eerily in the morning light. Two long, ebony horns curve upward from its skull behind its eye sockets. A short row of smaller horns juts from the top of her viper-like head. A long, forked tongue darts in and out of its mouth as it tastes the air.

"The wicked serpent seeks to devour them, commander," Præsidiel informs before slipping his helmet on. He looks over at Alex, who is setting his shield on the ground. The young knight begins tip-toeing toward the tower. "Wait. What are you doing, Commander?"

"Shhh." Alex makes a swatting motion toward the angel. "I'm gonna yank on its tail to get its attention."

"Will that not make it angry?"

"Course it will. S'what I'm countin' on. Gotta get its attention somehow. Once it finds out we're here, it'll come down after us. When it does, I'm gonna whack it on the head."

"Alexander, this is **not** an ordinary garter snake."

"I know. Still, we gotta get it away from the ladies up there, right? Just be ready." He continues to sneak up to the serpent's tail. He cautiously grabs hold of the tip of it with both hands. "Ooof. It's as heavy as those logs dad made me carry that one time." He whispers. Once he has a good grip, Alex positions himself. He takes a deep breath and then yanks the tail with all his might. He lugs it a couple of feet backward before slipping and falling on his rear end. He looks up to see the serpent whip its head around, gazing at them. "See. Told ya." He grins at Præsidiel, pointing to the serpent's head.

The beast glares down at the young knight with black eyes and piercing white pupils. Then, it slowly turns to slither back down the tower toward the knights. The boy knight's ploy worked. The serpent opens its gaping maw, hissing loudly. A smoky, fog-like mass bellows forth from its pitch-black mouth—two rows of needle-shaped fangs spring forward.

"Oh, snap!" Exclaims Alex. He jumps back to his feet and runs toward Præsidiel so fast he kicks up a dust cloud. He picks up his shield and, breathing heavily, says, "I think I cheesed it off."

"You certainly got its attention." Confirms the angel.

Alex draws his sword, which is a wooden picket, from a fence. He tightens his grip on the handle of his shield, a dented round metal trash can lid. He spreads his feet and crouches slightly. "You ready?" He asks, slightly bouncing in place.

"I am, commander." Præsidiel draws his glimmering crusader's sword slowly.

Eyes fixed on its enemies, the serpent's head barely moves as it slithers slowly toward the ground. Its darting, forked tongue tastes the air again and again. The giant snake stops as it nears them and rears its head. It knows Alex is the weak one, and quick as lightning strikes at the boy knight. Præsidiel deflects the blow with his crusader shield. Alex jumps to the side, narrowly dodging the poisonous bite.

Man, this thing is fast. He thinks. *I'm only gonna get one shot at this.* Though scared and wanting to run deep down, he stands his ground. The serpent raises its head to strike again. The boy throws down his shield and doubles his grip on his wooden sword. The serpent's tongue tastes the air while his body coils beneath him. Alex knows he's about to strike again.

Anticipating the beast's attack, Alex swings his weapon like a bat, landing a mighty blow to the side of the serpent's mouth. The impact hurdles the snake's head to the side and breaks one of its long fangs. Unfortunately, the shock of the strike breaks his sword and sends Alex flying sideways.

Præsidiel uses this opening to pierce the serpent's hide behind its jaw. He removes his blade, and it hisses and writhes in pain. Then, knowing it is beaten, the serpent spews forth a dark fog to conceal his escape. It turns and slithers away rapidly.

"Ow, ow, OW!" exclaims Alex, sitting on his bum and looking at his stinging hands. "Man, that hurt!"

Præsidiel runs to his side. "Are you okay, Commander?"

"Yes, sir. My hands are stinging, though."

"Well, I must say, your plan worked." Præsidiel sheaths his sword and extends his hand to the youth. "Forgive me, Commander."

"Course it did." Alex takes his angel's hand, who helps him to his feet. "Snakes are scared of you more than you are of them. You hit 'em in the head with a stick, and they'll always run." He makes a wiggly motion with his hand before dusting himself off.

"Yes, well, very courageous of you, Sir Alexander." The young knight nods in gratitude. "Now, we must call upon the princess and her maidens."

Alex blushes slightly. "I guess we should." He picks up his broken sword and dented shield. "You think God'll be mad I broke this sword."

"No, Commander. I do not think he will."

"All right then. Let's go check on the princess." Alex smiles and blushes again. "I hope she's pretty."

The two warriors climb the tower's stairs until they reach the apex. They knock on the door—the sound of a steel bolt sliding free echoes in the stairwell. Then the door is flung open by the beautiful princess. "Our heroes!" She exclaims.

Embarrassed, Alex lowers his head. She continues, "We witnessed your valor from our window. Truly, we are pleased to receive such brave knights. Please, come in. Rest." She motions with her hands, and her handmaids rush to prepare places for them to sit comfortably. "What is your name, good sir knight?"

"I'm Alex," he proclaims proudly, "and this is Præsidiel. He's a real live angel."

"Oh!" Answers the princess. "We are honored to welcome you, Sir Alex, the brave, and Sir Præsidiel, the holy." She curtsies and asks, "Please, may we offer you something to eat?"

"Thank you, your majesty." Alex makes a slight bow. The two take a seat at a small table. "I am kinda hungry."

The princess looks a little sad. "I'm afraid all we have to offer is bread and cider." One handmaid pours the cider into a cup while the other breaks a chunk of bread off for each.

"Most gracious. Most gracious indeed. Thank you." Says Præsidiel. He motions to Alex to take the cup.

The boy knight takes it. He sniffs at its contents before sipping it. "Oh,"–his words muffled by the cup–"this is delicious!" Alex sets the cup on the table and takes the bread. "Thank you." He noisily munches on the bread and, talking with his mouth full, says, "Did you see me yank on the snake's tail?" The princess smiles, and the maidens giggle as Alex regales them with his exploits. The angel watches and takes joy in the boy's happiness.

The conversation dies down soon after the young knight finishes his snack. "Don't know why, but I'm really tired all of a sudden. Must be that warm cider. You mind if I rest my eyes for a minute?" He asks, laying his head on the table. Alex is clearly exhausted.

"Please do, good sir knight." Says the princess. A hush settles over the tower. All is quiet as Alex falls asleep on his forearm.

Præsidiel stands. "Thank you, my lady, for your hospitality." He gently scoops up the wee knight in his sturdy arms. He unfolds his brilliant wings. "If you pardon us, I must return the lad to his chambers."

"Of course." She says. The princess curtsies, and her servants bow. "It was our pleasure, o holy messenger. We will pray for the boy and you. May God bless and keep him." The angel nods before gently taking flight out through the window.

Chapter 4:
Cap'n Alex

Alex wakes to the sound of whispering voices. At first, he's unsure if he's still dreaming or awake, so he lies still. It doesn't take long to feel the discomfort of the I.V. or realize the voices are not of the princess or Mr. Ray. Finally, he identifies the doctor's voice as he asks, "Has Alex been baptized?"

Lying still, Alex listens to his father's response, "No, but doesn't he already belong to God? I was always taught that a boy should be old enough to decide whether he wants to be baptized or not, that he must reach the age of discernment first. Why do you ask, anyway?"

"It is your decision, Aidan, but the boy's condition is deteriorating...rapidly." The doctor pauses. "Sadly, I don't think he will be with us much longer."

There is a silent pause after this statement, but Alex remains motionless, waiting, listening for more of the conversation. He doesn't realize his father dwells upon a memory of Alex. Aidan recalls a day not too long ago in his garage. Alex is picking up a piece of wood and some tools, distracting him from his work. "Alex, please put those down. What are you looking for, son?" Alex hastily put the tools back in place but unconsciously hung onto the wood. He remembers the innocence in the boy's eyes when he said, "I jus' wanna help dad." The youth's purity was not lost on his father either. He remembers smiling at him and saying, "Okay, son, hand me that piece of wood you have, and I'll show you what we're going to build."

Alex hears the voice of his mother call out, "Aidan." The boy opens his eyes slowly to see what is happening. He witnesses his dad looking deep into his mom's copper, tear-stained eyes. "Please, Aidan," she pleads. "We need to baptize Alex. We cannot put it off any longer. I know you believe it must be the child's choice to accept Jesus as the savior and be baptized, but isn't it our responsibility as his parents to ensure we have done everything to remove any sin? To prepare him as a gift to God?"

Aidan relents. He lets out a deep sigh. He takes her hands, "You're right, my love." He caresses Abila's face, wiping away her tears. "You're right. Call Father Soutane and ask him to come."

The doctor has noticed Alex is watching them. "Good Morning Alex." The doctor's voice catches his parents off guard. "I just popped in to see how you are doing today. You know, the nurses are still talking about your dream? Don't suppose you had another amazing adventure last night, did you?"

"Morning, Mom. Morning, Dad." He greets his parents as they regain their composure. Abila moves to his side. "I did go on another adventure last night." He states with muted excitement.

"Really?" asks his dad.

"Yessir. My angel," he pauses for a second, "you know, Mr. Ray? We had to fight a really big and scary serpent. I yanked on his tail and then whacked him in the snout. He slithered off, and we saved the princess." Alex smiles. "She was pretty and nice. We ate some yummy bread and drank some cider. It was delicious. I guess I fell asleep at the table, and Mr. Ray must've brought me back here."

"Wow! Now that is a dream." The doctor responds. "I bet the nurses would love to hear about this one too."

Just then, nurse Bonnie, Alex's favorite, enters the room. "Good morning Mr. Alex. How's my young adventurer this morning?" She winks at him before acknowledging his parents. "Mr. and Mrs. McBain." The family always enjoys her smiling face. "If you all will excuse me, doctor, may I speak with you for a moment?"

"Sure. By the way, wait until you hear Alex's latest dream." He nods at the boy and then follows nurse Bonnie out.

They pass through the door. Thinking they're out of earshot, nurse Bonnie says, "We have a small issue. The data you requested is incomplete. There was a 30-minute lapse in all our monitors last night." The door closes on their conversation.

Abila notices Alex has a few tiny breadcrumbs sprinkled on his blanket. "Sweety," she begins while brushing off the crumbs, "how did you get crumbs all over you?

* * * * *

As usual, the day came and went. After another day of unpleasant naps, hospital food, and uncomfortable silence, Alex finally got to sleep for the night, which was challenging considering his excitement at the prospect of a new adventure. However, tonight, Alex is finding it hard to remain asleep. It feels like his bed is moving, as though the ground is undulating beneath him. Furthermore, a strange light warms his face instead of the hospital lights' soft, cold glow.

Alex takes a deep breath and exhales. *I can't sleep*, he thinks. He slowly opens his eyes to find daylight beaming through oddly slanted oaken windows. He sits up, taking in his unfamiliar surroundings. There are cabinets next to shelves that have stacks of airtight bottles containing scrolls stored on them. A small desk and chair sit right in front of the windows. An hourglass, a feathered quill seated in an old inkwell, and paper are on the table. A dressing table sits in the corner, upon which a blue frock coat, gold waistcoat, and sword belt. Resting atop it all is a painted newspaper hat, which he instantly recognizes as the captain's hat he made last summer.

He looks down at the little twin bed upon which he sits. He's covered with a gray wool blanket. *Mmmm, warm but super itchy*, he thinks. There are two drawers underneath his thin mattress; one is halfway open. In it are another blanket and a brass spyglass. The headboard behind him is decorated with knotted rope and decorative lines. There is no doubt now. He has awakened aboard an old ship and is pleased to do so. Then there is a rap on his cabin door.

"Captain Alexander? Are you awake, sir?" Calls the unseen voice.

Happy yet groggy, Alex shouts back, "I'm up! I'm up." He rubs his eyes and smiles. Then he spins to his side to let his feet dangle off the bed. "Come on in."

A tall man bursts into his quarters. He is dressed in a similar, but less ornate, coat, tan pants, and white waistcoat, with a black kerchief tied around his collar. His hat is a short stovepipe shape with a flat and round brim. "We are in danger, Captain."

"Oh!" Exclaims Alex. "Mr. Ray. Good morning, sir." He greets while slipping on his stockings.

"Good morning, Captain. I have disturbing news."

"What's going on?" He asks, standing up and sliding his feet into his deck shoes.

"A pirate ship is gaining on us." He points out the window to a ship on their stern. "No doubt those scurvy buccaneers seek to board or sink our vessel."

Alex finishes dressing and quickly straps on his sword belt. He picks up the paper hat, sets it on his head, and smiles, "Ahhh. Still fits." Looking at himself in the mirror, he tugs at his coat. He thinks, *Now I look like a proper captain.* Then, satisfied he is ready for the battle, he turns to his first mate, "Show me the way, Mr. Ray." A giggle slips past his lips at the rhyme he just made.

The first mate escorts his captain topside. Together they rush to the helm of the 3-masted gunship. Alex looks over the main deck in awe at the HMS St. Michael, a First-Rate ship of the old British Navy. Ocean spray sprinkles his face, and the cooling wind refreshes him—the invigorating and overflowing energy of 9-year-old boy surges in his heart. Uncharacteristic of a regular sea captain, he looks out to his crew and enthusiastically salutes them by waving his paper hat in the air while shouting, "Ahoy, shipmates!" They erupt with a hearty cheer.

"Cap'n! Cap'n!" comes the call from the crow's nest. Alex looks up at the seaman there, who is pointing astern. "There, Cap'n, the ship what's 'bout to overtake us."

Alex turns and runs up to the quarterdeck railing. He produces a spyglass from his overcoat and looks astern at the ship. It's smaller, more maneuverable, and faster. He spots the Jolly Roger flying high and bold from the main mast. Scanning down the tattered and filthy sails, he finds a beastly man at the helm. He wears a black frock coat with silver buttons over a blood-red waistcoat. His dark gray pants are tucked into his black boots, with a cutlass on one hip and pistol on the other.

The pirate captain sees Alex looking at him. He momentarily steps to the side of the helm, removes his black and tattered tri-corner hat, and offers a sarcastic curtsy. Alex suddenly notices two horns protruding from the pirate captain's head as he stands back up. He places his hat back upon his head, covering them. His scraggly black beard blows in the wind as he parts his chapped lips in a wicked smile, exposing the rotten teeth behind them.

"Boy, he's ugly." The words slip unconsciously past his lips.

Mr. Ray whispers in his ear, "Aye, Captain, tis the devil that pursues us."

Alex lowers his spyglass. "Mr. Ray, ready the guns on the starboard side." He looks up at his first mate with a resolute grin. "We're gonna sink that mean ole' devil."

Cap'n Alex turns to his crew, pulls out his wooden sword, and, raising it in the air, shouts,

"Prepare the guns!" Another rousing cheer goes up. "Always wanted to say that." He says softly to Mr. Ray, who winks back at him.

"By your leave, sir, I will take it from here." Alex nods his approval. Mr. Ray begins barking orders, "Gunners, prepare the cannons on the starboard side. Master-at-Arms, Bo'sun, make ready the crew."

"Aye, aye!" They respond.

"Helmsman, starboard 20 degrees." Mr. Ray turns to Alex, "That should slow them down enough for the crew to make ready, Captain."

It isn't long before the devil's ship begins to pull alongside. Alex first notes their ship's blasphemous figurehead. He has seen many beautiful statues of the Mary, but this ship's insulting depiction of the Virgin Mother deeply offends and angers him. "Nobody mocks our Blessed Mother. We'll send 'em down to Davey Jones for that!" He mutters. He observes the motley crew. The devil's band of misfits swear and curse while waiving their cutlasses about. Some are shirtless, wearing only striped pants and black boots, with red sashes around their waists and bandannas covering their heads. Most are in tattered clothes and tri-quarter hats. Cannons thrust out through open portholes as the devil's ship swiftly pulls alongside.

Everything grows eerily quiet for a few seconds before thunder and smoke fill the air between the ships. The crew of the HMS St.

Michael duck and dodge as cannonballs whoosh overhead. The projectiles pass cleanly between the masts and rigging of the HMS St. Michael. Miraculously, the ship takes no damage. An unexpected wave caused the sea to swell at the right time. The crest raised the pirate ship just enough to make its cannons miss. However, the patience of St. Michael's gunner pays off. "FIRE!" he yells while they're in the trough of the wave.

Again the roar of the cannons shudders the air. Their volley strikes the pirate ship lower than planned, just above the waterline. The adversary's ship is rocked to the right before rolling back. It begins to list to the port side. "They are taking on water!" exclaims Mr. Ray.

A raspy and guttural voice carries across the water from the pirate ship, "I'll keel haul yuh from yer own vessel, yuh landlubber."

"Not today, you scallywag!" Cap'n Alex shouts back, shaking his sword at the adversary.

"Keep a sharp eye, me hearties!" cries the Bo'sun, pointing toward the adversary's rigging. "Scupper those bilge rats!"

Alex quickly glances out over the main deck to see what's happening. Several buccaneers swing on ropes from the pirate ship's rigging, trying to board Alex's vessel. One pirate swings across no man's land unseen, landing with his feet on the quarterdeck railing. He catches Alex by surprise. "Gotcha now, lad," snarls the dirty pirate staring down at him.

Alex freezes for a second. Mr. Ray realizes the scoundrel is still holding onto the rope he swung over on and is off balance. Alex snaps out of his fright and looks down to draw his sword. Mr. Ray leaps unseen toward the pirate. With a swift stroke, the first mate slices clean through the rope. Alex, not very tall, yanks his sword from his scabbard and smacks the feet of the would-be pillager, who falls backward into the ocean without the support of the rope.

He knows his senses are dulled, but he spied something odd as the raider falls backward. Alex quickly peers over the railing, sword still in hand, and notices a slender red tail with a point on its end swishing about just before the pirate plunges into the briny sea with a loud 'KER-SPLASH'!

Alex looks out over his ship to see what is happening. First, he witnesses his stout and steadfast crew repelling the enemy's boarding crew. A cutlass repels some, some are thrown over, and even one is blasted with a blunderbuss. Then, as the last one is kindly escorted off his ship, Alex points to the helmsman and yells, "Hard to port!"

"Aye, aye, Cap'n!" He confirms before spinning the ship's wheel.

Wind fills the sails of the HMS St. Michael. She pulls gracefully away from the sinking pirate ship. The devil curses and yells with fury. Again, in the very uncharacteristic manner of a naval sea captain, Alex turns aft and sticks out his tongue. "Nyah!" he exclaims. Afterward, he offers a cold shoulder to the would-be plunderers. He knows they're sinking, and their cannons cannot reach him. Cap'n Alex raises his sword high in the air in full sight of his crew, yelling, "Well done, me buckos!"

The crew throws up their arms and shouts in victory.

"Mr. Ray."

"Aye, Captain."

"Best adventure yet! However," Alex exhales deeply, "I'm feeling really tired all of a sudden." He sheathes his sword just in time to cover a giant yawn with his hand. "Let's find a port. I'm sure the crew could use some shore time." He adjusts his hat, informing, "Think I'm gonna go back to the cabin."

"Aye, aye, sir. Helmsman, steady as you go until we can get the proper bearings."

"Aye, aye," the helmsman acknowledges.

Alex stops at the top of the ladder to witness the HMS St. Michael sailing into the expanding amber and vermillion sky. The sun is setting. The smell of gunpowder and the sounds of battle fade in their wake. The smell of the sea, the sounds of the ship plying its waters, and the rocking motion soothe the young captain. The Bo'sun sings a shanty while the crew works in rhythm, cleaning the boat, handling lines, and returning her to good order while others keep watch. The Quartermaster takes new bearings and gives commands to the helmsman. Though tired, Alex feels a deep sense of satisfaction and joy.

He starts down the ladder toward his cabin. Mr. Ray accompanies him. "You have accomplished much as a brave young sea captain." He opens the cabin door. "Forgive me for reminding you, but Captains must log their day's activities and seal them in a bottle."

"Uhg!" Alex rolls his eyes. "Seriously! Homework?"

"I will prepare your desk while you get comfortable, Captain."

"I'm sorry, Mr. Ray. I'm just tired, is all." Alex says while sluggishly undoing his sword belt and kicking off his shoes. "You're my new best friend. You know that, right?"

"It is my pleasure, *Captain* Alexander." Mr. Ray picks up the parchment, grabs a bottle, and places everything on the desk. "A thought before you make your logs." Alex throws his frock coat on the dressing table and turns to listen respectfully to his angel in disguise. "Life ebbs and flows on a tide. Some days the swell will raise you, and others, you will find yourself down in the trough. Either way, my good friend, you must be thankful to God and sail ahead boldly."

Alex rubs his eyes. "That's pretty deep there, Mr. Ray." He gives a sudden coy smile as he sits at the desk. "Just like the ocean."

"Aye, captain." Mr. Ray chuckles. "That it is. That...it...is." He grabs the blanket from the bed and gently lays it over Alex's back. "To keep you warm, sir. Now, by your leave, I will see to the crew."

"Thank you, shipmate." Alex smiles as his friend departs.

"Aw man, why do I have to do this?" the boy grumbles. "After an adventure like that?" He grudgingly takes the quill in hand, dips it in ink, and begins to write. He only gets a few words entered into his log when exhaustion takes hold. He places his arm on the table and lays his head on it. He tries to keep writing, but his eyes are too heavy. Moments later, a child's snore can be heard coming from the captain's quarters.

Chapter 5:
Sheriff Alex, the Kid

Sunlight warms his face, and a subtle chatter fills his ears. A groggy Alex wakes in his hospital bed. He is not alone. There is a small crowd in his room. His mother, father, and Sitti are there, as always, but so are a couple of first responders, nurse Bonnie, her husband, and a man in a black cassock. His grand tales of fighting fires, defeating serpents, and hanging out with an angel are reaching the ears of many. Inspired by the joy with which he faces a life-threatening illness, they have come hoping to hear another grand tale.

Alex, emaciated and weak, struggles to sit up in bed. Bonnie moves swiftly to adjust it, so he doesn't have to labor. "Thank you." He says before rubbing his eyes. It takes him a second, but he finally recognizes the man in the black robe. "Father Soutane?"

"Ah, you do remember me. God bless you, lad."

"Course I do. You're my mom's favorite priest. She says good things 'bout you." Father Soutane glances at Abila and smiles. His mother blushes. "They tell yuh about Mr. Ray; I mean Præsidiel? That's his real name. How he's a real angel?"

"Yes, they did." He says as he moves to Alex's side. "Sounds like you're in good company." He winks at the boy. "And I'm guessing you've been on another adventure?"

"Oh, yes, sir. You wanna hear about it?"

"Yes, of course, but in due time, my young explorer." The priest's tone takes on a more serious tone. "First, do you know why I'm here?"

"Well, I heard my mom 'n dad talkin' about baptism yesterday, so I'm guessin' you're here to baptize me."

"You are a smart young man, Alex. That is precisely why I'm here." He leans closer, "I'm sure your angel, Præsidiel, will be most happy when it's done too." He winks at him again.

"Okay, father. I'm ready then."

"Well then,"—he lightly claps his hands together—"let's get started." Father Soutane greets everyone present officially. He briefly reminds them of the joy with which the parents welcomed this child as a gift from God and then moves on to the ceremony. "You have named this child Alexander. Now, what do you ask of God's Church for him?

"Baptism." Aiden and Abila reply in unison.

"And the grace of Christ and eternal life." Add Sitti and Alex's mother.

Father Soutane turns toward nurse Bonnie and her husband. "I understand you are to be his godparents. Are you ready to help his parents in their Christian duties?"

"We are." They also state in unison. Based on his surprised yet happy look, they could tell Alex was surprised by the announcement. He likes nurse Bonnie, who has become a close friend of their family over the last few weeks. Tilting her head slightly, she offers Alex a warm smile.

"Alexander, the Christian community welcomes you with great joy. I claim you for Christ our Savior by the sign of his cross. I now trace the cross on your forehead and invite your parents, your Sitti, and your Godparents to do the same." The priest signs the child on the forehead. The rest follow his example.

"Due to the circumstances, we will celebrate with an abbreviated reading from the apostle Mark." Father Soutane motions for everyone to sit and be comfortable. He reads from Mark 1: 9-11 (the baptism of Jesus) and Mark 10: 13-16 (let the little children come to me). Next, he gives a short homily on Luke 2:21-40 (the presentation of Jesus in the temple) and the trust the Blessed Mother and St. Joseph had in God. He notices Alex's heavy eyes and says, "Let us profess our faith." Everyone in the hospital room recites the Apostle's Creed in a low, whispering tone.

"Now, let us prepare for Alex's baptism." The movement in the room reinvigorates the boy. Father Soutane readies the holy water he brought. Abila moves to the boy's side to help lift him while his dad stands near the head of his bead. Nurse Bonnie slightly lowers his bed, gathers a towel, and stands beside his mother.

Once they're all in position, Father Soutane begins the baptism from the opposite side of the bed. "Alexander, I baptize you in the name of the Father," the priest gently pours the water over Alex's head. He stops momentarily as some of the water runs down his forehead. A nervous giggle slips out of the boy. "and of the Son,"–He pours the water a second time and again pauses–"and of the Holy Spirit."–He pours the water over his head a third and final time.

Alex is wide awake now. His new Godmother raises the bed while Father Soutane puts away the water. His mom dries his face and head with the towel, and his dad helps him get comfortable.

The priest returns to the bedside with a bottle of oil. He says, "God the Father of our Lord Jesus Christ has freed you from sin, given you a new birth by water and the Holy Spirit, and welcomed you into his holy people. He now anoints you with the chrism of salvation. As Christ was anointed Priest, Prophet, and King, so may you live always as a member of his body, sharing everlasting life."

Everyone in the room responds, "Amen."

Father Soutane dips his thumb in the bottle of olive oil mixed with balsam. Its fragrance immediately fills the room as he again traces the Sign of the Cross on the boy's forehead, saying,

"Alexander, be sealed with the gift of the Holy Spirit."

Though he's only a boy, Alex feels a sense of relief, of peace. An effervescent thought fills his young mind; *Everything is going to be okay.* He knows his life's story will end happily, and his heart soars with joy. He understands the gift he has just been given, enthusiastically responding, "Amen."

His response is received with light applause from everyone in the room. Family and visitors crowd around to congratulate him while Father Soutane packs the ceremonial items. Then, as things settle down, he returns to Alex's side. "Now," he says with a wink and a smile, "how 'bout that adventure?"

Rejuvenated, Alex scooches up in his bed and tells the tale of his battle at sea, the roar of cannon fire, and fighting off scurvy pirates. He beautifully describes sailing into the setting sun. He expresses his awe of the ship and her crew. He even laments being tasked with homework.

"My goodness, lad!" Father Soutane says, jumping to his feet. "I wish I could've been right there with you." The priest, acting as though he had a sword in hand, waves his hand, saying, "I'd've helped you scupper those brigands too." Alex giggles. The priest suddenly realizes he's probably a little too excited. "Ahem. Well then." He pauses to regain his composure. "How did you get back here?"

Alex shrugs, "I guess the angel keeps bringing me back after I go to sleep."

"Hmmm..."–Father Soutane glances toward Alex's parents and then back to Alex–"Let's hope he keeps bringing you back to us." He gives the boy a fond smile, which Alex happily returns, nodding. "It has been a pleasure, young man. However, I must get back to the parish and God's work." He collects his things and prepares to depart. He pauses as he passes the foot of the bed, asking, "May I come back to hear more of your stories?"

"Yes, please." Alex delightfully confirms.

"I look forward to it. Until then, Alex, may God bless and keep you, always." He waves and smiles at all those present. Aidan rises to escort him out. They whisper as they exit. Alex only hears something about the reconciliation and sacraments.

Afterward, the day's routine slowly returns. Visitors and nurses come and go. His dad comes back for a moment before heading off to work. Abila feeds her young adventurer lunch, though he is only capable of eating half of it. However, he saves just enough room for the sweeties Sitti sneaks him when nobody's looking. Alex slides in and out of catnaps over the course of the day. Unfortunately, his discomfort and naps are noticeably more frequent than before.

Alex's parents return in the evening to find him staring out the hospital window. Typically, the evenings grant father, mother, and son quiet solitude from the rest of the world. They would much rather be gathered around the kitchen table instead of eating supper around Alex's bed. Regardless, they usually discuss the day's happenings, but tonight there is a palpable and uncomfortable feeling of numbness in each of them. The encroaching finality renders them silent for most of the evening. Nevertheless, for now, there is a simple unspoken pleasure in being in one another's company.

Alex groans with discomfort as he turns to lie on his side for a bit. As he does, Bonnie returns. She has started her shift and wants to check on her new godson. Her heart breaks at seeing the pain behind his heavy eyes. She kneels between his parents, "Mom, Dad, I hate to say it, but it's getting late. Visiting hours are almost over. We need to take his vitals and make Alex comfortable for the night."

"C'mon, Bonnie. We still have time." Aidan protests.

"S'okay, Dad," Alex interjects before letting out a big yawn. "I'm really tired anyway. 'Sides, I wanna get some rest before Mr. Ray comes tuh get me."

Parental love and instincts create a reluctance to leave, even now. However, the deep trust they have in their nurse assuages their fears. "Okay, little buckaroo. You get some sleep. We'll see you in the morning. Until then, I know Mrs. Bonnie will take care of you."

He hasn't heard his dad call him that for some time. A contented Alex sleepily grins. "Love you, Dad. Love you too, Mom."

"Oh, my sweet darling, I love you. You mean the world to me. Sweet dreams." Abila leans over and kisses her son softly on the cheek.

"Love you too, Son." His dad winks. "Be safe on your next adventure."

Nurse Bonnie politely ushers mom and dad out of the room. When she returns, she finds the brave young boy fast asleep. She quietly sets to the work at hand. She straightens his room, checks his I.V., inspects the monitors, and tucks him in. As she does so, she accidentally kicks something under his bed. The distinct 'clink' of a glass bottle rattling there perks up her ears.

Hmmm, she thinks, *I wonder if Father dropped his bottle of chrism oil.* She stoops to look under the bed. She finds an old bottle, not at all like the one the priest used. It's a little misshapen, like it was handblown. It's a sea green color with an old cork in the end. "Now, where in the world did this come from?"

She notices a piece of old parchment inside the bottle. She removes the cork, which makes that familiar 'pop' sound, upends the bottle, and shakes the note to its mouth. "Aw, c'mon," she mutters when it doesn't come out. She pinches at the message with her fingertips. Finally grasping enough parchment to pull, she gently removes it, turns it over, and quietly reads the child-like scribble, "Thank you God for." The sentence ends abruptly.

She looks at Alex. *It can't be*, she thinks to herself. *How'd he get out of the bed, much less the hospital?* She stuffs the note back into the bottle. After replacing the cork, she slips it into her pocket. "Someone's havin' a laugh at my expense." She scoffs.

* * * * *

Alex wakes to someone nudging his arm. "Sheriff. Wake up. There is trouble." He slowly stirs. Unable to see, he realizes there is a hat over his eyes. His feet slip off the desk they once rested on, and his leaning chair flies forward, landing on all four legs. Wide awake from the sudden lunge forward, he grabs the hat off his head and inspects it. It looks like the one his dad brought back from a trip to Wyoming once. He always loved it when his dad would place it on his head. It's one of his favorite hats. He smiles and puts it back. A little oversized, it falls to his ears.

He looks around and realizes he's in some old west jailhouse. Two cast-iron cells on either side of the jail's half-open front door stand out against the simple, wood-clapboard walls. Before he can finish checking his surroundings, the man beside him says, "Sheriff. We have trouble." Alex looks up, immediately drawn to the silver, 5-point badge on his tan waistcoat. He turns his gaze back to his own coat. He slides his thumb behind the lapel and lifts it to inspect the circular badge surrounding a 5-point star pinned there. "You hear me, Sheriff?"

"What? What's all the fuss about?" Asks Alex.

"El Diablo and his gang are down at the Bartlett Inn. They have come for old Polly's soul." Deputy Ray points to the apparition floating in the cell on the right. A transparent, gaunt-faced woman with black hair is in the middle of the cell. Her once-white dress and dark blue, button-downed shirt fade and shimmer. The woman's spirit sways and moans.

"Yikes! Is that...a real ghost?" Alex exclaims as he jumps to his feet. "Never seen a real ghost before." He adjusts the oversized hat on his head, peering at the specter from under its brim. "She sure is creepy."

"That is the ghost of Polly Bartlett. She murdered many men in her day. Her soul is trapped here, awaiting judgment. El Diablo has come to claim her." Mr. Ray pauses briefly before repeating, "He and his gang are at the Bartlett Inn. I must warn you, Sheriff; he is mean enough to steal the coins off a dead man's eyes, as they say."

"I know. I've heard he's one mean hombre, but I ain't 'fraid of him. You know why Mr. Ray?"

Alex pats the receiver on his lever action BB gun. "'Cause I got Ole Betsy with me. I'm a pretty good shot too." He then points to Deputy Ray's side arms and continues, "Besides, you got them Colt peacemakers. 'Tween you and me; we can take 'em, pardner."

At that very moment, a deep, raspy voice echoes through the dusty western town, "Sheriff Alex! I'ma callin' you out, boy!"

"Welp,"–Alex clacks the lever on Ole Betsy, cocking the gun–"guess it's time we mosey on out there and face the music." He winks at Deputy Ray. "Let's run that varmint outta town."

In agreement, Mr. Ray tugs at the brim of his hat, "I am with you, Sheriff."

Alex pulls the door open and walks out into the hot summer sun. He stretches in the warm light. "Man, I'm sore." As he walks into the town's main street, his boots crunch on the dry, dusty ground. A tumbleweed blows past, and the silence becomes deafening. Then, finally, he stops to observe his surroundings. "Where is everyone?" He mumbles.

"This is a ghost town, Alexander." Confirms the angel.

As his friend speaks, Alex notices a single man standing in the middle of the street. The young sheriff turns to stare him down. A wide-brimmed black hat shades the man's dark eyes. His pointed beard and handlebar mustache hide the scowl of his curled lips. His deep crimson waistcoat stands against the foil of his long black duster coat. He wears a full bandolier over his shoulder with another gun belt on his hips. He has two pistols holstered there. Alex instinctively raises his blue-steeled BB beauty to his side.

"Whaddaya think you're gonna do with that li'l pea shooter?" The desperado turns his head and spits on the ground.

"Maybe I'm gonna shoot yer eye out."

The bandit gives a hearty laugh.

Mr. Ray leans toward Alex, "Watch out, sheriff. He's got one on the roof of the old General Store and one hiding by the Inn." Alex nods his gratitude but keeps his focus on the outlaw.

El Diablo slowly reaches for his guns. "You have one of mine in there, Sheriff, and I aims to bust 'er out." Then, he growls, "No yellow-bellied, snot-nosed kid's gonna stop me, either."

"Hold it right there,"–Alex raises his rifle and aims–"you old son of a gun," Alex commands. Although he has a firm grip on his pistols, El Diablo hesitates to draw them. It's a standoff. If it wasn't for the light wind stirring up the dust, Alex swears he could hear showdown music from some old spaghetti western playing in his ears.

Flinching, El Diablo moves to draw his revolvers. Alex squeezes the trigger of Ole Betsy. Two sounds break the peace, 'KA-PAP,' followed by a light 'thunk.' The devil drops his guns and clutches his face. "Holy @#$%*! He shot my eye out!" He kneels in the road, screaming with rage, "Get 'em, boys!"

Deputy Ray pulls his Colt peacemakers with lightning speed and jumps in front of Sheriff Alex just as two bullets strike the dirt on either side of the boy. He fires a round from each of his pistols, hitting the would-be assassins with deadly accuracy. El Diablo's assassins burst with an ectoplasmic explosion when struck by the bullets.

Just as fast as it began, the shootout is over. Alex and Mr. Ray run toward El Diablo with their guns trained on him. Alex cocks his trusty sidearm again. Deputy Ray kicks the outlaw's guns out of reach. "Go on. Git!" Alex shouts before mumbling, "You old sidewinder." He raises his voice again, "Less you wanna lose the other eye!"

Clutching his bad eye with one hand, El Diablo points to the lawmen, "I'll be back to get her one day 'n there's nothin' you can do about it."

"I said, go on."

The devil looks at Mr. Ray, who motions for him to go with one of his pistols. "You heard the sheriff. Depart from us." El Diablo turns and grudgingly leaves town. The two lawmen watch him until he disappears over the hillside. Once he is out of sight, the angel holsters his pistols and turns to his young friend. "Well, I do not think he will return for some time. You did a great job, Sheriff."

Alex lowers Ole Betsy. "We sure showed him, huh?" He raises the brim of his hat. "Yessir. I've been enjoying these adventures with you, Mr. Ray. But, I gotta tell yuh, it's getting harder and harder to do 'em. I just keep getting so tired so easy." He takes a deep breath and exhales. "I feel so weak all the time."

"You are tired because your journey is nearly at an end." There is an uncomfortable silence as they stroll on. "Are you ready, Alexander?"

"Whaddaya mean? To go back to the jail and check on ol' Polly?"

Mr. Ray shifts his form, losing his western attire and taking on his angelic appearance. "No, Alexander, are you ready for what is to come?"

"Oh," Alex says sadly. "That."

The two turn back toward the Old Sweetwater Jail. "You are weak because the illness has taken its toll on your body and mind. As such, this was our last earthly adventure," states Præsidiel.

"I understand." Alex drags his boots on the dusty road. The little sheriff looks up at his angel, the brim of his hat almost covering his eyes, "Do I still get to see my mom and dad one more time?"

"Yes."

The young man quietly smiles as he turns his gaze back to the ground before him. Upon entering the old jailhouse, Alex notices the bed in the empty cell has been turned down with lush sheets and blankets not found in the wild west. He doesn't care that it's out of place, however. Instead, the boy lumbers toward it and sits down on the edge of the bed. He leans Ole Betsy against the headboard, takes his hat off, and places it over the barrel of his trusty BB gun. Then he kicks off his boots and crawls under the covers. "Sure am…tired." He is unashamed about not covering his big yawn. "But I wanna see Mom & Dad again."

Alex's guardian angel tucks his special ward in. "Sleep well, Alexander, for the next time I am sent to you…." his voice trails off.

Chapter 6:
A Warrior's Welcome

Alex hears his mother's quiet prayers. Lying still with his eyes unopened, he feels the weak heartbeat in his chest. It's weird, but he could swear it beats in cadence with his mother's prayers. He feels the I.V. in his vein and the chill of the solution running up his arm. The sensors on his chest itch and pull at his youthful skin. He doesn't want to move because he knows it will be painful if he does, so he slowly opens his eyes. His mother stops praying.

"Good morning, my beautiful boy." She greets.

Alex exhales before saying, "Good morning, Mom." He smiles at her. "Where's Dad?"

"He stepped out for a few minutes but will be right back."

"Momma?" Alex asks with a weakened voice.

Abila wraps her rosary around her wrist and approaches her son. "Yes, my darling?" She gently takes his hand.

"Mr. Ray said last night was my last adventure. I...I think...it may be time for me to..." Alex passes out.

His mother frantically pats the boy's hand. "Alex! Alex!" she screams. His heart monitor beeps in an odd pattern. "Nurse. Nurse." Her cries escalate.

A nurse rushes into the room, quickly assesses the situation, and hits the call button for help. "What happened?" She asks.

"I don't know. He was talking and then just passed out."

Another nurse and a doctor rushed into the room. Abila is gently squeezed out of the way by the tending physician. They administer oxygen and check Alex's vitals, among other things, to stabilize him.

Aidan bursts into the room and quickly envelops his wife in his arms. "What happened?"

"Alex just collapsed while he was talking." Tears stream down her face. "Oh, Aidan. I'm not ready to lose him yet. I'm not..." she sniffles. He offers no words, for he has none himself. So instead, she turns her face into his chest, hiding within his strong embrace.

* * * * *

When Alex opens his eyes again, he sees Father Soutane before him. He is groggy and unsure. He looks slowly around to discover his mom and dad next to him. Extremely weak, he lifts his hand, which his mother readily takes in her own. "Sorry...Momma."

"Oh, baby, it's okay. I'm here. I'm here."

His dad brushes Alex's hair back and caresses his head. "You gave us quite a scare."

Alex sees the restraint in his father's eyes.

"Dad?"

"Yes, Son?" He continues to stroke his hair.

"I...I think it's time...time tuh go meet Jesus." Aidan can no longer hold back the tears; they flow freely. He chokes back his emotions. "That's why we asked Father Soutane to come." He glances in the priest's direction. "He's here to offer you viaticum, last rights"–he sniffs and wipes his eyes–"so you can go to Our Lord."

Alex shifts his head slowly to the right, turning his attention to Father Soutane. "Whadda I gotta do?"

"Don't worry, young Alexander; I'll take care of everything." He moves to the table set up at the foot of the bed. There are two small candles, a vase, and a small cloth. Father Soutane solemnly removes a pyx from the burse around his neck. He gently places it on the table, genuflects, and rises again. Then he takes a rod with a ball on the end of it out of the vase.

"What's that?" Asks Alex.

"An aspergillum. We use it to bless with holy water." The priest sprinkles first the boy with the shape of a cross. Alex smiles briefly when the cool water lands on his cheeks. Then he sprinkles some on the floor around his bed, the room's walls, and those gathered around. When he is finished, he returns the aspergillum to the vase.

Then, turning to everyone else, he informs, "I am truly sorry, but I have to ask everyone to step out of the room for a moment so I can hear Alexander's confession."

Though it was expected, everyone reluctantly exits into the hospital hallway.

Father Soutane pulls up a chair and sits next to Alex. He wants to be at eye level with the boy. He looks into Alex's sunken eyes and gaunt face. He knows his time is limited.

"Father, I don't know how this works."

"It's okay, Alex. All I want to ask is if there is anything you might have done in your life that you are sorry for. Get into a fight? Disobey your parents? Things like that."

"Well...there was one time when I pulled Suzie's hair. I felt awful bad 'bout that. I punched Tommy once too. He broke my favorite action figure. I lied to Momma when I took some cookies, and Dad too when I broke his tape measure and hid it."

"Are you sorry you did those things?"

"Yessir. I love my momma...and my dad. I wish I could take back what I did tuh my friends, too."

"Is there anything else?"

"No, sir. Not that I can think of."

"That was a good confession, Alex. For your penance, I want you to say a Hail Mary."

"Like my mom says?"

"Yes, dear one, like your mother says." The priest grants him absolution, "...through the ministry of the Church, may God give you pardon and peace, and I absolve you from all your sins in the name of the Father, the Son, and the Holy Spirit."

Alex joins Father Soutane in saying, "Amen."

"You have been forgiven, Alex. Now, you say your Hail Mary, and I'll call everyone back." He gets up, moves the chair back, and goes toward the door. He takes much delight in hearing the lad repeat the prayer from memory.

Aidan, Abila, Sitti, Bonnie, and a few of the hospital staff re-enter. Mom and Dad immediately go to his side.

"Momma, I said the same prayer you say all the time, the Hail Mary." She smiles at him. "Maybe I'll meet her too when I get up there."

"Oh, my darling, I hope so." Tears stream down her face. "I hope so." She caresses his sunken cheeks.

Once everyone is settled, the priest goes to the table, genuflects again, rises, and then uncovers the pyx. He picks up the open pyx and carries it to stand next to Alex's bed on the opposite side of his parents. There he prays before taking out the consecrated host. Then, holding the pyx in his left hand under the eucharist, he offers the consecrated host to Alex.

Alex's eyes dilate immediately after he consumes it. The room changes. Several angels appear around the room, each standing behind those who came to see him. He recognizes their faces. They were the EMTs on the scene in his first adventure, the two servants in the tower, and his faithful shipmates on the ship. The walls beyond begin to fade.

In the distance, a tan and white stone wall gradually materializes. In the middle of it is a fifty-foot tower extending into a pre-dawn sky. At its center are two arches, one external and one recessed. Two elegant stone lions are carved on either side of the archway. Massive oak doors, ornately decorated, seal the entrance. Small shrubs and grasses spring up around his former hospital room. Hints of a vast wilderness between the wall and a gleaming city on a faraway hill tease his curiosity.

His distant stare scares his mother. "Alex. Alex, baby. What are you seeing?"

"Mom. Dad." Alex's voice grows faint, but his eyes refocus. He turns his head toward them. "Don't be 'fraid. You…you gotta let me go." His eyes dilate again, and he returns his view toward the distant wall. "See…there's a…a great expedition for me…in heaven. One to 'scover Jesus." Although his parents try to hold back their sobbing, their tears flow freely. "He's waitin' for me, Momma. We get to explore together…Him 'n me."

The angel Præsidiel appears at the foot of the bed. Only Alex can see him and hear his call. Alex lifts his hand to wave. Those gathered look around, trying to see whom he's waving at. "Are you ready, Alexander?" Asks the angel.

The dying boy nods slightly, "Yessir, Mr. Ray." His voice is fading to a whisper, "I'm...ready." Alex's eyes close slowly.

The heart monitor flat lines. The room grows silent.

* * * * *

The remnants of the hospital, the world itself, disappear. It takes a moment before Alex's eyes adjust to the blinding white light. Appearing before him is a small group of people. Beyond them is an endless and vibrant wilderness waiting to be explored. Still coming into focus is a great, shining city that rests on a distant mountain. Alex turns his eyes back to the group forming a semi-circle before him.

The two men on the left wear light blue tunics with white linen togas. To their right is an American Indian Chief dressed in tan animal skin pants, and a pale-blue shirt, with a large, feathered headdress on his head. Sitting on his shoulder is a curious little man. Alex has seen pictures of Japanese warriors wearing the same clothes, but this man is much smaller, about a foot tall. Next to the chief is a black man wearing blue denim coveralls over a white linen shirt. On his head is a faded blue forage cap with a black brim, like the Union soldiers wore in the civil war. They're all smiling at Alex, who looks curiously at the angel beside him.

Two more small, winged Japanese warriors fly toward the group. One is a man, the other a young woman wearing an ornately blue kimono. The man lands on the Chief's other shoulder while the young woman lights gracefully on the Præsidiel's shoulder. She smiles at the angel and then turns to offer a polite bow to little Alex.

"Please, Alexander, allow me to introduce you." Offers the angel with an open palmed point. "This is Ioannes, Cælius, and Hania. On his right shoulder, Takeda-san, and on his left, Hasegawa-san." Præsidiel looks down at Alex and says with a wink, "We sometimes call him 'Wrestles with Hare.'" The others chuckle. "To their right, Samuel, a patriot from your own country. He, of all these fine warriors, knows exactly what your parents endure, but that is for another time. And lastly, but certainly not least, here on my shoulder, the brave Ashi-hime. These Alexander, are some of my friends. Each a warrior in their own right." Alex politely nods and smiles at them. "Everyone," continues the angel, "this is Alexander 'the great'"—he winks at the boy—"our newest, and youngest, warrior." They gather around to pat him on the shoulder, say hello, or offer a bow, welcoming him.

After the warm welcome, the angel puts his arm around Alex and leads him through the group. "Now, my young friend, you see what lies at your journey's end. However, before we go any further, there is one you must meet." As everyone makes way, Alex is unexpectedly met by a man and a woman. The tall, strong man stands slightly behind and to the woman's right. He has the appearance of a wise and gentle father. He gives Alex an affirming nod. The woman is dressed in a flowing, silken white gown. Over that is a royal blue mantle trimmed in gold and adorned with golden floral patterns. A white veil, trimmed in lace, cascades from her head past her shoulders. Around her waist is a gold belt and cincture. On her head is a crown with 12 stars. She radiates light as bright as the sun. Alex instantly recognizes her.

"Mother Mary?" Alex asks shyly, unconsciously twisting his bare toes in the dirt.

"Yes, child."

"I knew it was you." Shouts Alex. "It just had to be." He runs to her exuberantly.

She squats down, spreading her hands wide to embrace him as only a mother can. Alex rushes into her arms. "Oh, my child, I am so happy to see you." She pats him, "You are such a brave young man." She holds him out to look at him and smile. He sees the same deep love in her eyes as he has always seen in those of his earthly mother.

"Hope you don't mind me sayin', but you're way more beautiful than I imagined." Alex's cheeks flush.

Joseph pats Alex on the shoulder and smiles warmly at him while Mary continues, "We are only here to welcome you briefly." Alex cocks his head at the curious statement. She gazes over his shoulder, looking beyond him. "Even now, I hear your earthly mother's cries and your Sitti calling out to me." She returns her eyes to the boy and smiles. "They call to me on your behalf."

Though he is reluctant to turn away from her majestic and loving beauty, Alex looks over his shoulder. He is surprised at the sight of his mother holding tightly to his hand and weeping. His earthly dad stands beside his body, looking down at his only son with tremendous sorrow.

Alex turns back to the immaculate face of Mary. "I don't understand." He says with curiosity.

"Oh, my child. It is not your time," Mary answers lovingly. "Your earthly journey is not quite at an end."

* * * * *

Though the sun blazes through the hospital window, the otherwise silent room is filled with weeping, sobbing, and sniffling. Abila feels an unexpected twitch in Alex's hand. She raises her eyes in shock. "Beep, beep...beep, beep," the heart monitor sounds again. Aidan looks at the machine first, then at Alex, whose eyes open slowly and blink. "Mom? Dad?"

Chapter 7:
Astronaut Alex & the Space Ogre

Alex's mother stands at the kitchen sink, doing some dishes and looking out the window into their lush backyard. There is a raucous racket upstairs. Her mother, Sitti as she is known, sitting at the table with her tea, inquires, "Abila, what in the world are those two doing up there?"

"If I know Aidan, he's probably roughhousing with Alex." Then, a deep-throated "RRROOOAAARRR!" reverberates through the house, immediately followed by a boy's scream, "Ahhhh!" Next, they hear the sound of tiny footsteps as they patter quickly across the floor above.

Young Alex comes thundering down the stairs, bounds over the ottoman in the living room, and rushes into the kitchen, where he is confronted by his mother, "Whoa, whoa, whoa there!" She exclaims. Alex's sneakers screech to a halt on the linoleum floor. An oversized space helmet bobbles around on his head. "Who do you think you are, Spaceman Spiff?" She asks with a grin. "What planet do you think this is?" Sitti is doing her best not to snicker at his appearance.

Alex lowers the ray gun in his right hand and lifts the visor on his helmet with his left. "I'm not

Spaceman Spiff, mom. I'm astronaut Alex!" He declares. "I've gotta get back to the moon base and protect it from the space ogre who's chasin' me." The sound of purposefully heavy footsteps falls on the treads in the stairwell, followed by another loud "RRROOOAAARRR!"

"Goodness me, what is that?" Asks Sitti.

"That's the space ogre I was warnin' yuh 'bout, Sitti. He's chasin' me and is gonna attack the moon base," exclaims Alex. "I gotta get outta here."

"Well then, I guess you better hurry. On your way, Astronaut Alex," Says his mom.

"Yes, ma'am." He slams the visor shut on his helmet and bolts for the back door. He opens the door and warns, "Y'all better find a place to hide, too, or he'll getcha!"

Just then, Aidan stomps into the kitchen. His arms are raised like Frankenstein's monster, and he is wearing a pair of old springy antennae on his head. He bellows, "I'm gonna eat yuh, scrawny spaceman."

Alex takes aim with his ray gun and says, "Nuh, uh! Take this! Pew pew!" He then runs out the door toward his backyard treehouse. The screen door slams closed behind him.

Aidan lowers his arms and laughs. "Ladies," he greets them with a smirk. Sitti smiles, shakes her head, and sips her tea. Then, he raises his arms back up and grabs Abila. "Grrrr. Pretty spacewoman."

She squeals and smacks playfully at him.
"Don't you have a moon base to attack…space ogre?" She laughs.

Aidan dips his wife, and the antenna on his head bounces. He kisses her. "Don't you worry, fair space maiden; I'll destroy that base." He stands her back up and releases her. He looks over at Sitti and smiles mischievously. "Ma'am." He nods.

Sitti rolls her eyes, smiles, and says, "Boys…."

Aidan walks over to the back door. He throws it open and yells, "RRROOOAAARRR! Must destroy moon base!"

A faint voice calls back from a distant treehouse, "No, you won't!"

Space ogre roars again before stomping out into the backyard, letting the door slam behind him. Sitti takes her tea and joins her daughter at the sink. "It was so good to see **all** of you at Mass on Sunday." She says, standing next to her daughter.

"Yes. Yes, it was." Abila drapes her towel over the edge of the sink and opens the kitchen window. The fresh air wafts in. She takes a deep breath. "Mmmm," she exhales with a contented moan. Placing her hands in front of her on the sink, she stares out the window at her boys. Together, she and her mother watch the legendary battle for the moon base unfold.

"So, his illness is completely healed?" Sitti asks before taking a sip of her tea.

"Yes. The doctors have no explanation for it either, Mom. It's just...gone."

"A miracle then," Sitti states with certainty.

"It would seem so." A deep sense of peace enters her heart as she stares out the window. Bright-colored flowers dot the verdant landscape. She watches a breeze move across the grass and then rustle the leaves in a tree on its way toward the kitchen window. The gentle wind caresses Abila's skin and brushes her hair. It also causes a bottle on the sill to wobble.

Sitti sets her tea on the counter before reaching for the sea-green container. "Where'd you get this?" She inquires, gently taking the bottle in hand.

"Bonnie gave that to us on the day we checked Alex out of the hospital." Abila looks at her curious mother, who is inspecting it. "She found it the night before Alex...." She doesn't want to finish the sentence.

"There's a note inside." Sitti rotates the bottle. "It's kind of scribbly." She gasps when holding it up in the light. "Is this Alex's handwriting?"

"Yes." Abila's eyes fill with tears. "Go ahead, read it."

"Thank you God for." She turns it looking for more. "It just trails off," she notes.

A teardrop escapes from the corner of Abila's eye. "Yes." She sniffles before continuing, "Thank you, God."

"Yaaarrrg!" Alex's fearsome scream interrupts their moment of peace.

The ladies turn their attention to the backyard. They look out just in time to witness Astronaut Alex leap fearlessly over the railing into the space ogre's arms, who subsequently, and very overdramatically, falls to the ground. Unscathed, Alex jumps to his feet, "That'll teach yuh to invade my moon base, ogre!"

"Aahhhk! You got me, spaceman!"

Mother and daughter giggle at the boys playing in the backyard. Sitti replaces the bottle on the windowsill. She wraps her arm around her daughter. "Yes, Abila, God is good."

A loving family has been made whole, and once again, all is right in the world.

"But Jesus looked at them and said, "With men it is impossible, but not with God; for with God, all things are possible." Mark 10:27

About the Author

John Eudy is a twenty-six-year military veteran. He was a soldier in the Army National Guard and a 'shallow water' sailor in the U.S. Coast Guard. Although not as well-traveled as the wayfarer rat, he has at least been around the block a time or two. He has cautiously wandered the lava fields of Kilauea, snowshoed to the summit of Cadillac Mountain, strolled among giants in King's Canyon, and swam with wild dolphins in the Gulf of Mexico, which he naïvely thought were sharks at first sight. He even traveled through time once … by making a round trip across the international date line to visit Guam.

These days, John and his family reside smack-dab in the middle of America. He has been married to his lovely wife of nearly 30 years, and they are the proud parents of four daughters, two of whom are already with God in heaven.

Inspired by faith and scripture, he enjoys weaving history, cultural legends, personal life experiences, and Christian morality into fictional novellas.

OTHER BOOKS BY JOHN EUDY

A Glorious Day in Hell:
The Day Jesus Descended

Guardian of the Lightning Seeds

Legacy of Lightning:
Rise of the Hotaru Onna-musha

Morning Glories & Moonflowers

Made in the USA
Monee, IL
01 May 2023

32672218R00049